Mr. Strike Out

BY JAKE MADDOX

illustrated by Sean Tiffany

text by Anastasia Suen

Librarian Reviewer
Chris Kreie
Media Specialist, Eden Prairie Schools, MN
M.S. in Information Media, St. Cloud State University, MN

Reading Consultant
Mary Evenson
Middle School Teacher, Edina Public Schools, MN
M.A. in Education, University of Minnesota

 STONE ARCH BOOKS
Minneapolis   San Diego

Jake Maddox Books are published by Stone Arch Books,
A Capstone Imprint
1710 Roe Crest Drive
North Mankato, Minnesota 56003
www.capstonepub.com

Library of Congress Cataloging-in-Publication Data
Maddox, Jake.

Mr. Strike Out / by Jake Maddox; illustrated by Sean Tiffany.
p. cm. — (Impact Books. A Jake Maddox Sports Sstory)
Summary: David is a great baseball pitcher, but he always strikes
out at bat until he learns about Babe Ruth and the importance of
practice.

ISBN-13: 978-1-59889-061-7 (library binding)
ISBN-10: 1-59889-061-1 (library binding)
ISBN-13: 978-1-59889-239-0 (paperback)
ISBN-10: 1-59889-239-8 (paperback)

[1. Baseball—Fiction.] I. Tiffany, Sean, ill. II. Title. III. Title:
Mister Strike Out. IV. Title: Mr. Strikeout. V. Series: Maddox, Jake.
Impact Books (Stone Arch Books) Jake Maddox Sports Story.
PZ7.S94343Mr 2007
[Fic]—dc22   2006006077

Art Director: Heather Kindseth
Cover Graphic Designer: Heather Kindseth
Interior Graphic Designer: Kay Fraser

Printed in the United States of America in Stevens Point, Wisconsin.
112011
006455R

Table of Contents

Chapter 1

Yankees vs. Lions

Twelve-year-old David Gray, a pitcher for the Yankees Little League team, stood at home plate with a bat in his hand.

I have to hit the ball, thought David, or I'll never hear the end of it. Carter is on third, waiting to come in, and we already have two outs.

David studied the Lions' pitcher. He watched the pitcher wind up.

It was a slider! David swung the bat.

Wump! The ball landed in the catcher's mitt.

"Strike one," said the umpire.

Here we go again, thought David.

David watched as the pitcher looked over at third. Yeah, yeah, I see Carter too, thought David. And if I don't bring him home, he'll give me an earful.

The pitcher looked at home plate. First the windup, and then the ball flew toward home plate.

Another fastball. Hit it! David swung.

Wump! "Strike two," said the umpire. The pitcher looked at home plate and nodded his head.

Here it comes! thought David. It was a change-up this time.

David swung as hard as he could.

Wump! "Strike three! You're out!" said the ump.

The Lions ran off the field. Mark Carter sprinted over to David as he walked toward the parking lot.

"Can't you do anything right?" said Mark. "No wonder they call you Mr. Strike Out!"

"Give him a break," said Andy. "They only call him that because he's a strike-out pitcher."

"But he strikes out all the time, too," said Mark. Mark looked at David. "I haven't seen you hit the ball once."

"Lighten up," said Coach. "We won the game."

"Okay, Dad," said Mark. Then he turned and gave David a dirty look.

"Good game, Dave," said Coach.

"Thanks, Coach," said David. He took off his batting helmet.

"Good game," said Andy.

"Maybe," said David.

"Maybe?" said Andy as he took off his catcher's gear. "We won, and you say maybe it was a good game?"

"I know," said David, "but I can't hit the ball."

"Don't let Mark bother you," said Andy. "Everyone knows that he's got a big mouth."

"But he's right," said David. "I never hit the ball."

Chapter 2

Practice

Two days later David stood on the pitcher's mound. The Yankees were practicing on their home field.

Mark was batting, and Andy was catching as usual. Andy signaled a change-up. David nodded his head, and then he wound up. The ball flew through the air.

Mark swung his bat at the ball.

Wump! Andy caught the ball.

"Dad!" yelled Mark. "He's trying to strike me out."

Coach came over. "Good," said Coach, "that's what I want him to do."

"But I can't hit the ball," said Mark.

"That's what David does," said Coach. "You're not supposed to be able to hit his pitches."

"But how can I practice batting if I can't hit the ball?" said Mark.

"Well," said Coach. He looked around the field. Over by third base Tyler was pitching to John, the assistant coach.

Coach put his fingers to his lips and whistled. Wheeet! "Hey, Tyler! Come over here and pitch for a while."

"Okay, Coach," said Tyler.

Coach looked at David. "You can warm up with John for a while."

"Sure," said David. He looked back at Andy. Andy rolled his eyes.

Mark is the coach's son, thought David. He's always whining about something. As long as I get to pitch, that's all that matters.

David walked off the mound and went over to the grassy area by third base. John was Andy's older brother and the third base coach. "Throw me all the strikes you want," said John.

"Great," said David.

"Here's the ball," said John. He threw a ball to David.

"Thanks," said David.

John crouched down. David wound up and threw the ball. Wump! "Good one," said John, and he threw the ball back. "That was right in the strike zone."

Wump! "Another strike," said John and he threw the ball back. "Give me a fastball this time."

"Okay," said David, "one fastball coming right up." David moved his fingers by the seams and wound up.

Wump!

"I can really tell you've been practicing," said John. "But what about your batting?"

"My batting?" said David.

"You seemed pretty upset about striking out the last game," said John.

"Oh, that," said David.

John walked over to David. "Are you practicing your batting, David?"

David looked up at John. "Uh, no."

"Why not?" asked John.

"Well, I stink at it," said David. "So I just do what I'm best at. Everyone likes my pitching."

"You're a great pitcher," said John, "but batting is part of the game too."

"But pitchers don't bat," said David.

"Not in the American League, they don't," said John, "but that's a few years away. What'll you do in the meantime?"

David kicked at the grass, hard. "I don't know."

Chapter 3

The Babe

"I have two words for you," said John. *"Il Bambino."*

"What?" said David.

"Il Bambino is Italian. It means 'the baby,'" said John.

"It was Babe Ruth's nickname. Babe Ruth is the most famous baseball player who ever lived!" added John.

"Oh," said David.

"He was a pitcher," said John, "who was also a batter. In fact, he was a home run king!"

"Well, uh," said David.

"I'm not saying you have to be a home run king," said John.

"I can't even hit the ball," said David.

"All you need is a little practice," said John kindly.

"Coach wants me to practice my pitching," said David. He looked over his shoulder. Coach was watching them.

"So we will," said John. "Just remember the Babe."

"Uh, okay," said David.

"Come on. Throw me another fastball," said John.

David moved his fingers over the seams and wound up. The ball flew into John's mitt.

"Another strike," said John. "That's really great!"

After practice David rode home with Andy and John. They were going to have pizza at Andy's house.

"I was telling David about the Babe," said John.

"Here we go again," said Andy.

"What?" said David.

"I've heard this story a million times," said Andy.

"I can't help it that I'm a history nut," said John.

"Nut is right," said Andy.

"You go look up Babe Ruth on the computer. I'll make a pizza," said John.

"Uh, okay," said David.

David sat in front of the computer. "What was that name again?"

"Babe Ruth," yelled John from the kitchen. Andy rolled his eyes.

"Thanks," said David. He typed "Babe Ruth" into Google.

"You should find a million entries," said John as he entered the room.

"What about the pizza?" said Andy.

"It's in the oven," said John. "We'll eat in fifteen minutes."

John pointed at the computer. "Click this one," he told David.

David clicked on the link.

"Babe Ruth," said John.

"Wow!" said David. "It says Babe Ruth was one of the first five players elected to the Baseball Hall of Fame."

"Yeah, and he started out as a catcher," said Andy.

"Then he was a pitcher," said David.

"He played in the American League," said Andy.

"And he batted?" said David.

"They didn't have a designated hitter in those days," said Andy.

"That's prehistoric!" said David.

Chapter 4

Yankees vs. Mustangs

David picked up a bat and walked out to home plate. How had things gone so wrong?

He thought, I didn't let a single Cardinal on base when I was pitching. But today, in just three innings, the Mustangs scored six runs!

David looked out at the field. Mark was on second, and Ryan was on third. John was coaching third, as usual.

John gave David a thumbs-up.

I'm not a batter, thought David. I'm a pitcher. I just can't do both.

The Mustangs pitcher nodded his head. He wound up. David swung with all his might.

Wump! The ball hit the catcher's mitt.

"Strike one," said the umpire.

Here we go again, David thought. The pitcher looked over his shoulder. Mark moved back to the bag.

The pitcher looked over at third. Stop stalling! David felt like yelling. Ryan is standing on the bag.

The pitcher looked at David, nodded his head again, and wound up. It was a change-up. David waited just a second.

Then he swung. Wump!

"Strike two," said the umpire.

Not again! David looked back at the dugout. "You can do it," yelled Andy.

No, I can't, thought David. I really can't. The pitcher nodded his head. Another fastball! David swung.

Wump!

"Strike three," said the umpire.

The Mustangs jumped in the air and cheered. They ran up to the pitcher and gave each other high fives.

They won. The Mustangs won because of me! David thought.

Mark ran up to David.

"Can't you do anything right?" said Mark meanly.

Coach came out of the dugout. "Good try, David," he said.

"But, Dad," said Mark, "we lost because of him."

"David wasn't the only player in this game," said Coach.

"But he struck out," said Mark.

"And when you dropped that ball, a runner scored," said Coach.

"The sun was in my eyes," said Mark.

"So, no one's perfect," said Coach. "Come on, let's go."

David watched as they walked away. If Mark is going to All-Stars, he thought, then I am too.

I have to learn how to bat!

Chapter 5

After the Game

"Hey, John," said David. "Wait up!"

John put down the bag of bats he was carrying out to the car. "What's up, David?" said John.

"Um, can you teach me how to bat?" asked David.

"Sure," said John. He reached into his back pocket and took out his cell phone. "Call your mom and tell her you're coming to our place for pizza again."

"Okay," said David.

After they ate some pizza, David, Andy, and John drove back to the park for some batting practice.

"I'll catch," said Andy as they got out of the car.

"Good," said John, and he threw Andy a mitt.

Andy caught it. "This isn't my catcher's mitt," he said.

"I know. We're going to use the tee," said John.

"The tee?" said David. "We're too old for T-ball."

"I know," said John, "but not too old to hit the ball."

"What?" said David.

John put his hands on David's shoulders. "David, you're a pitcher, right?" said John.

"Uh, yeah," said David.

"So when you come up to bat, you study the pitcher, right?"

"Of course I do," said David.

"Well, that's your problem right there," said John.

"What?" said David.

John took the tee, the bag of bats, and the ball basket out of the trunk. "You're still thinking like a pitcher," he said. "I want you to think like a batter."

"Think like a batter?" said David as they walked out to the field. "How do I do that?"

John put the bag of bats and the ball basket down. Then he walked over to home plate and put the tee on it.

"A ball for the tee, please," said John.

"Okay," said David. He took a ball out of the basket and put it on the tee.

"Go way out, Andy," said John.

"I know the drill," said Andy. He ran to keep outfield. "Ready!"

"Okay," said John. "David, step up to the plate."

David took the bat and stood next to home plate.

"Now look at Andy," said John.

"I see him," said David.

"Okay," said John, "now send him the ball."

"Uh, all right," said David. He swung the bat, and the ball flew into the outfield.

Andy caught it and threw it back.

"How did that feel?" said John as he caught the ball.

"Good," said David. "I like hitting the ball way out there. It feels good."

"That's what I want to hear," said John. He went over and picked up the ball basket.

"I don't need that many balls," said David.

"We're going to keep Andy busy," said John. "I'll put them on the tee and you'll hit them."

"Uh, okay," said David.

"Hey, Andy," said John. "Here they come."

"Bring it on," said Andy.

John put a ball on the tee, David hit it, and in a few minutes the basket was empty.

"I could use a little help out here," said Andy as he ran around the outfield picking up balls.

"We're on our way," said John, and then he turned to David. "You hit every ball into the outfield!"

Chapter 6

Yankees vs. Frogs

Say good-bye, thought David as he wound up.

The ball landed in Andy's mitt before the batter finished swinging.

"Strike three!" said the umpire.

The inning was over. David ran back to the dugout.

"Great job!" said Coach. He patted David on the back.

Mark made a face but didn't say anything. He picked up a bat and walked out to home plate.

"You're up after Mark," said John.

David took off his cap and put it on the bench. Then he put on a helmet and picked up a bat.

"Have you been practicing your batting?" asked John.

"Every day after school," said David.

"Good," said John.

Crack! David and John looked out at the field. Mark had hit the ball out to the fence! "That's at least a triple," said John, smiling.

David watched Mark run to third. Coach stood next to first base clapping his hands.

"Good job, Mark!" yelled Coach. "David!" he said. "You're up!"

David looked at Mark on third. Here we go again, he thought.

David walked over to the home plate.

I can do this. I can do this, he reminded himself.

David watched the pitcher wind up.

It's a fast ball. David swung.

Wump! The ball hit the Frogs' catcher's mitt.

"Strike one!" said the umpire.

The catcher threw the ball back to the Frogs' pitcher.

The Frogs' pitcher nodded his head and wound up.

It's a change-up! David swung.

Wump!

"Strike two!" said the umpire.

David looked over at third base. Mark was frowning at him, but John gave David a thumbs-up.

I can do this, David thought.

The Frogs' pitcher wound up. The ball flew toward home plate.

Crack! David hit the ball, and it went straight up into the air.

"Run!" yelled Coach.

David dropped the bat and ran toward first base.

"Good try, David," said Coach when David reached first base.

"Did Mark score?" said David.

"No," said Coach. "It was a pop-up."

"He caught it?" said David.

"Yes," said Coach, "but it was a really nice try."

But it didn't count, thought David as he slowly walked back to the dugout.

Chapter 7

Batting Averages

At practice on Tuesday, Coach asked David to warm up with John.

"I can tell you've been practicing your batting," said John as he threw the ball to David.

"I might as well have struck out," said David. He threw the ball to John.

"No," said John as he caught the ball. "You at least hit the ball."

"But I was still out," said David, "so what does it matter?"

"What does it matter?" said John. He walked over to David and asked, "Who said you had to be perfect?"

David looked up at John. "Uh, no one did, I guess."

"So why are you so hard on yourself?" said John. "Even Babe Ruth struck out sometimes."

"Well," said David.

"Come on," said John. "That's what batting averages are all about. Sometimes you hit the ball and sometimes you don't."

"And sometimes you hit the ball, and you're still out!" said David. He stared down at the grass.

"Yes, that happens sometimes," said John kindly.

"The angle was all wrong," said David. "That's why it went up instead of going forward."

"That makes sense," said John.

"But how can I practice for that with a T-ball stand?" asked David. "The ball is always in the same place when you use a tee."

"True," said John.

"So I'll never learn to hit the ball," said David.

"Well, I wouldn't say that," said John. "You just need to try something new."

"Like what?" said David. "I can't hit the ball when someone pitches it to me. So what's left?"

"Tennis," said John.

"Tennis!" said David. "I don't want to play tennis! I want to play baseball."

"Now hold on a minute," said John. "Look over at the tennis courts."

"Okay," said David. "I'm looking."

"What do you see?" asked John.

"People in white clothes running after a yellow ball," said David.

"There it is," said John, "third court over. Watch the guy on the right."

"Watch him do what?" said David. "He's just standing there."

"Give him a minute," said John.

David watched as the guy threw the yellow tennis ball up into the air.

Then he hit it with his racket, and the ball flew over the net.

David turned to look at John. "That guy threw the ball," said David, "and then he hit it."

"Exactly," said John. "I think that's your next step."

"But I'm not playing tennis," said David. "I'm a baseball player."

"But the movements are almost the same," said John. "Look at Coach."

David turned around. "He's at home plate," said David.

"Right. Just watch what he does next," said John.

"Okay," said David.

Coach threw the ball up in the air, and when it came down, he hit it with his bat. The ball flew into the outfield. Mark caught it.

"Good catch, Mark," said Coach. "Now, Travis, here's one coming your way." Coach threw another ball up into the air, and when it came down, he hit it to Travis on second base.

"How does he do that?" asked David. "How does he hit the ball exactly where he wants it?"

"Practice," said John.

David laughed. "I knew you were going to say that."

Chapter 8

Yankees vs. Hawks

David stood at home plate. The score was Hawks 3, Yankees 4.

We're ahead of them, thought David, but I still want a hit.

The Hawks pitcher nodded his head. Then he turned around and checked out the bases.

David looked over at third. John was coaching third base. He gave David a big thumbs-up.

The pitcher turned all the way around. Mark was near second base. He moved back and touched the bag when the pitcher looked over at him.

David wiggled his bat. Okay, he's back on base. Can you pitch the ball now? he thought.

The pitcher turned back to home plate. He nodded his head again.

Just throw it, thought David.

Finally the pitcher wound up and threw the ball.

It's a fastball! David swung.

Crack!

The ball went straight up in the air. David dropped the bat and ran toward first base.

"Nice try," said Coach when David reached first. "But it was foul."

David walked back to home plate. Here we go again, he thought. He picked up the bat and looked at the pitcher.

The pitcher nodded his head.

David held the bat tighter.

The pitcher wound up.

It was a change-up. David swung the bat hard.

Crack!

The ball flew through the air.

David dropped the bat and ran toward first base.

David touched the base and turned around. The pitcher stood on the mound with the ball in his hand.

"Another foul ball," said Coach.

"Not again," said David. "That makes it two strikes!"

"It was barely over the line, David," said Coach.

David walked back to home plate again. He picked up the bat and looked at the pitcher.

The pitcher looked at the catcher and nodded his head. David gripped the bat. The pitcher wound up.

It's a wild ball! David jumped back so the ball wouldn't hit him.

The ball flew past the catcher and the umpire and hit the fence.

The catcher ran after the ball and threw it back to the pitcher.

The pitcher caught the ball and looked over at the dugout. The Hawks coach had come out of the dugout.

Don't change him now. I only need one more pitch, thought David.

The Hawks coach nodded his head and touched his ear. The pitcher nodded his head.

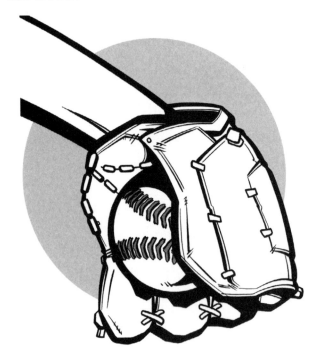

Hmm. What signal is that? David moved back to home plate.

The pitcher wound up.

It's a low ball. David swung at it.

Crack!

Wump! The ball flew straight into the pitcher's mitt!

I hit it right to him! Man, I give up, David thought angrily. Forget about batting. Forget about All-Stars. Forget about Mark and his big mouth.

I've had enough!

Chapter 9

Bad Pitching

David walked slowly over to the Yankees' practice field.

"Hey, David," said Coach. "You warm up with John again, okay?"

"Okay," said David. He walked over to John.

"Hi, David," said John. "Have you been practicing?"

"No," said David. "What's the use? I get out every time."

"You hit the ball when you came up to bat in the last game," said John.

"Yeah," said David, "two foul balls!"

"That wasn't all you hit," said John.

"I hit the ball right into the pitcher's mitt," said David. "That didn't count."

"It didn't count?" said John.

"It wasn't a hit," said David. "When someone catches the ball it's an out."

"So that means it's bad?" said John.

"If I can't score," said David, "why should I bother?"

"Only home runs count?" said John.

"Well, no," said David.

"Your batting has improved a lot," said John.

"But I can't hit during the game," said David. "It's easy to hit the ball on a tee, or when you throw it yourself. But when someone pitches it to you, it's a lot harder."

"So that's the next step," said John. "We'll pitch to you."

"But I'm the pitcher," said David, "and Tyler is warming up with Coach."

"And Andy's just sitting around," said John. "Hey, Andy!" Andy came over. "Coach said he wanted you to catch for a while."

"Perfect," said John, "because I want you to pitch to David."

"But he's the pitcher," said Andy.

"He needs to learn how to bat," said John.

"But I'm a lousy pitcher," said Andy.

"David needs to learn how to hit bad pitches," said John.

"Then I'm your man," said Andy.

John threw Andy the ball. "Pitch him a slow one."

Andy wound up and pitched the ball to David.

Crack! The ball flew up in the air.

"That was another fly ball," said David sadly.

"But you hit it," said John. "That's what counts."

"It doesn't count when they catch it," said David.

"They don't always catch it," said Andy kindly.

"Well," said David.

"Whether they catch it isn't up to you," said John. "All you need to worry about is whether you put it into play."

"I'll go stand in the outfield," said John, "so the ball doesn't go over into the other field."

"I can't hit it that far," said David.

"We'll see," said John.

"Hey, batter, batter," said Andy. "Here it comes."

Crack! David hit the ball, and it flew into the air. Whap! The ball landed by second base. Andy walked over to pick up the ball.

"Leave it there," said John. "I want to see where he's hitting them."

"Okay," said Andy. He walked back to the mound and took another ball out of the basket. "Are you ready?"

"Ready," said David.

"Here it comes."

Crack! The ball flew up and landed in left field.

"Way to go!" yelled John.

Maybe I **can** bat, thought David.

Chapter 10

David walked up to home plate. Here we go again, he thought. I didn't let a single man on base when I was pitching. But things changed when it was Tyler's turn to pitch. The Wolves scored three runs to the Yankees' two.

David put his bat up and looked at the Wolves pitcher.

The pitcher nodded his head, and then he turned around.

Mark had stepped off the bag at second base.

He's not going anywhere, thought David. Ryan is still on third.

As if on cue, the pitcher looked over at Ryan on third.

David wiggled his bat. "Throw me the ball," he whispered.

The Wolves pitcher turned back and nodded his head. Then he wound up and threw the ball.

A fastball. David swung. Crack! The ball flew straight up. David ran to first base. Then he looked at Coach. "Was it a foul ball?" asked David.

"Yes," said Coach. "Just out of reach of the catcher."

"Okay," said David, and he walked back to home plate. I have to hit it out, not up!

David picked up the bat and stepped up to the plate. The pitcher nodded and then wound up.

Change-up, thought David. He swung hard at the ball.

Crack! The ball flew out to third base. David dropped the bat and ran to first base. He touched the bag and turned around. Ryan was still on third base!

"Why didn't Ryan run?" David asked.

"The ball went over the line by third," said Coach.

"Another foul?" asked David.

"Only by a few inches," said Coach.

"Not again," said David.

"I'm sure you'll hit it in this time," said Coach. "Your batting keeps getting better."

"Do you think I can make it to All Stars?" said David.

Coach smiled. "We'll see."

"Okay," said David, and he walked back to the plate. This is it. I have to hit this one so I can make it to All Stars.

David picked up his bat and stood by home plate. He looked the Wolves pitcher in the eye. Throw me a fastball, he thought.

The pitcher nodded his head and wound up.

It was a fastball.

David swung with all his might.

Crack! The ball flew out toward third base. David didn't even look. He just dropped the bat and ran toward first.

As he reached first, Coach said, "Keep running!" So David ran to second.

As he reached second, David heard John yelling, "Keep running, David!" So David ran to third.

When David touched third base, John said, "Stop here."

Panting, David turned around to look at the field.

The catcher had the ball in his mitt.

"Give me five, Babe Ruth," said John. He put out his hand. "David, you just hit a triple!"

"A triple!" said David. He slapped John's hand.

"And two RBIs," said John. "You hit both Ryan and Mark in."

David looked over at the scoreboard. Wolves 3, Yankees 4.

No more Mr. Strike Out!

About the Author

Anastasia Suen is the author of more than seventy books for young people. She played left field when she was in school. Anastasia grew up in Florida in the early NASA days and now lives with her family in Plano, Texas.

About the Illustrator

When Sean Tiffany was growing up, he lived on a small island off the coast of Maine. Every day, from sixth grade until he graduated from high school, he had to take a boat to get to school. When Sean isn't working on his art, he works on a multimedia project called "OilCan Drive," which combines music and art. He has a pet cactus named Jim.

Glossary

ball (BAWL)—in baseball, a pitch that does not cross home plate between the batter's shoulders and knees

base (BAYSS)—in baseball, a base is one of the four corners of the diamond to which you must run in order to score

change-up (CHAYNJ-up)—a slower pitch made with the same motions as a fast pitch

fair (FAIR)—by the rules

foul (FOUL)—a ball hit outside of the foul lines around the playing area. The foul lines are drawn from home plate to first and third bases.

slider (SLY-dur)—a fast pitch that curves away from the batter

strike (STRIKE)—in baseball, a pitch counted against a batter

triple (TRIP-uhl)—in baseball, a hit that allows you to reach third base

wind up (WYNDE up)—the movements a pitcher makes before he throws the ball

Further Info

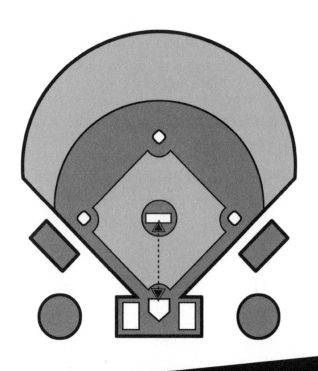

Little League players use a sixty-foot diamond. The distance from the pitcher's mound to home plate is forty-six feet. When players move up to Junior League, the size of the diamond increases to ninety feet. Junior League pitchers throw the ball sixty feet and six inches!

About Baseball!

The strike zone is the area over home plate between the batter's armpits and knees. In this picture of David, the strike zone is the gray box.

Discussion Questions

1. The main character, David, always worries what Mark will think about him. Why do you think he does this? What advice would you give David?

2. Has your coach helped you play better? Andy's brother, John, spends a lot of time helping David. Why do you think he does this? Has an adult, like a coach, ever helped you with something?

3. Why do you think it was so hard for David to hit the ball?

Writing Prompts

1. If you play baseball, how did you learn to bat? What about another sport you might play? What was a hard skill you learned?

2. Have you ever struck out at bat? Have you ever practiced really hard at something and still not done well, like studying for a test? Write and tell how you felt about it.

3. David is hard on himself because he can't always hit the ball. If you had a friend like David, write down what advice you would give him.

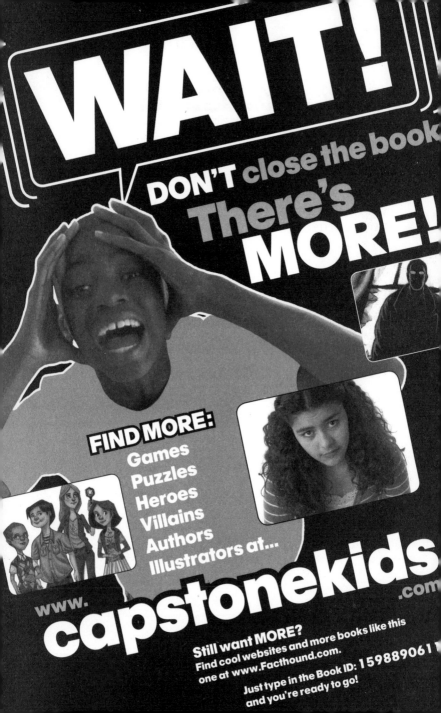